Robert Barclay

AF130243

On Membership in the Society of Friends

Anatiposi

Robert Barclay

On Membership in the Society of Friends

Reprint of the original, first published in 1872.

1st Edition 2023 | ISBN: 978-3-38215-370-0

Anatiposi Verlag is an imprint of Outlook Verlagsgesellschaft mbH.

Verlag (Publisher): Outlook Verlag GmbH, Zeilweg 44, 60439 Frankfurt, Deutschland
Vertretungsberechtigt (Authorized to represent): E. Roepke, Zeilweg 44, 60439 Frankfurt, Deutschland
Druck (Print): Books on Demand GmbH, In de Tarpen 42, 22848 Norderstedt, Deutschland

ON

MEMBERSHIP

IN THE

SOCIETY OF FRIENDS,

BY

ROBERT BARCLAY.

BEING SOME REMARKS ON AN ARTICLE LATELY PUBLISHED IN THE

"FRIENDS' QUARTERLY EXAMINER,"

ON BIRTHRIGHT MEMBERSHIP,

By JOHN STEPHENSON ROWNTREE.

LONDON:

SAM^L. HARRIS & CO., 5, BISHOPSGATE STREET WITHOUT

SESSIONS, YORK. SCOTT, CARLISLE. PENNEY, DARLINGTON.

IRWIN, MANCHESTER. WHITE AND PIKE, BIRMINGHAM.

WHEREAT, BRISTOL. EDMUNDSON, DUBLIN.

PREFACE.

THE writer of this paper had no intention ever to have addressed his fellow Members upon the subject of Birthright Membership. An article, however, appeared in the *Quarterly Examiner* of Fourth Month, 1872, from the pen of his friend and valued correspondent, J. S. Rowntree, in which he endeavoured to stem the growing conviction of some of our most active and valued Members, that Birthright Membership is at the root of some of our greatest difficulties —a view which was shared by our friend J. S. Rowntree himself in 1859, and expressed to the world in his well-known Prize Essay. It should be clearly understood that the writer considers this fact to entitle his friend's arguments in favour of Birthright Membership to our most careful consideration, and that it in no way places him at a disadvantage, although allusion to it in this pamphlet is inevitable.

Incidentally, statements, similar to those which the writer has made publicly with reference to the nature of Membership in the early Society of Friends, are controverted in the article lately published in the *Quarterly Examiner ;* and, most reluctantly, after carefully considering the subject, he feels bound by considerations of his duty towards the Society, to reply to this article as a whole, and particularly to bring forward some facts connected with Membership in the early Society of Friends, which he did not intend to publish in a controversial form.

He ventures to think that the view taken by J. S. Rowntree— that Membership in the early Society of Friends was a Birthright Membership—is not only shown to be untenable, but that the contrary may be considered to be fully established.

The full discussion of the subject of our present system of Membership could hardly be opened better than by a defence of our existing position by so able a writer as J. S. R., and the impossibility thus exhibited of defending it on any principles but those which, if carried out to their legitimate conclusion, would destroy (if it were possible) the Visible Church, and her *united* testimony for Christ in the midst of an ungodly world, has convinced the writer that it is the duty of all who love the great principles of the Society of Friends, seriously to consider if it is possible to prepare the way for a new and better system of Membership.

SOME REMARKS UPON J. S. ROWNTREE'S ARTICLE ON "MEMBERSHIP IN THE SOCIETY OF FRIENDS,"

Published in the "FRIENDS' QUARTERLY EXAMINER" of Fourth Month, 1872.

CHAPTER I.

On the Membership of the Early Christian Church—The Controversy between the Donatists and the Catholic Church, and the Membership of the Church of England.

MOST of our readers will remember the "Parable of the Bread-fruit Tree" in the ingenious and able "Short Studies on Great Subjects," by J. A. Froude, the historian. It vividly depicts the fate of great institutions reared by the virtue, and maintained by the energy, of a generation of far-sighted men. It is told something after this fashion:—

"The men with clear heads and brave hearts ploughed and harrowed the earth. They observed one plant larger and fairer than the rest. Its flowers were so fragrant and its fruits were so valuable that many others of mankind came and gathered under it, and those who had raised it received them with open arms. They made their homes under the shade of its branches which stretched over the plain, and rejoiced in its loveliness.

"The tree grew stronger and fairer, and they and their children's children watched it, age after age, as it lived on and flowered and seeded. But they took no care of the seed. The scent of the flowers and the sweet fruit were all they thought of, and they said, 'The tree is *immortal*, it will never die.' The wild birds and beasts of the field caught the stray fruits and seeds, and bore them away, and scattered them in far-off soils.

"At last the tree began to cease to grow, and then to droop and fade. Its leaves were not so thick, its flowers were not so fragrant; then a branch fell. But the men who lived under it denied that it was not what it once was. At last there could be no doubt that the leaves were thin and that the fruit was tasteless. But the generation was passed away who had known the tree in its beauty, and so men said it was always so—its fruits were never better, its foliage was never thicker. So things went on, and strangers would come among them and say, 'Why are you sitting here under the old tree? There are young trees grown of the seed of this tree, far away, more beautiful than it ever was; see, we have brought its leaves and flowers to show you!' But the men would not listen. They were angry.

"At last, some of *their own wiser men* brought out specimens of the old fruits, which had been laid up to be preserved, and compared them with its present bearing, and they saw the tree was not as it had been, and such of them as were good reproached themselves and said it was their own fault. They had not watered it, and had forgotten to manure it. So then, like their first fathers, they laboured with might and main. This was only partially successful, and they grew weary and looked for a shorter way. They tried grafting from the shoots which the strangers had brought. This did not answer, and then they tied on the preserved fruits to the tree; but there were not enough, so they supplemented them with leaves and fruit and flowers of wax and clay. Their little children were taught to hold their tongues about it. If the little ones and the weak ones believed, it answered all purposes. But some saw that this was not honest and truthful conduct, and passed out in search of other homes under the shade of the young trees grown of the seed of this tree, far away."

We leave our readers to apply the moral, if there be any, and to consider whether there are any portions of the parable which apply to the present state of the Society of Friends. We think if it be so, that J. S. Rowntree, in his able Prize Essay on the Causes of the Decline of the Society of Friends, may be considered one of the people who showed us that the Society was once a flourishing tree, and clearly proved to us its decline. One of the characteristics of this Essay was that it was full of reasons why the tree was dying, but contained no clear instructions to the people who dwelt under it, as to the right course to be taken. He told us there were causes for its decline, which were the result of human apathy, of faulty methods of culture; that the seeds of the tree were not reared into fresh, young and vigorous trees, with all the care and skill which the value of such a tree demanded. He told us in the Essay that Birthright Membership was one of the main causes of the decline of the Society. The effect of this rule of the Society was that the old tree was depended upon, instead of the natural and divine method of renewing the old tree being taken advantage of. The digging about the roots and manuring the old tree had been neglected, because the men had not the experience which they would have had if they had been constantly engaged in rearing young trees. We may add that it was once the fashion to deprecate the rearing of young trees, because it was said "they produced nothing but leaves." Then came a period when some praised the cultivators but forced them to adopt methods of cultivation which were ill-adapted to the end desired, instead of acknowledging that they had no experience to guide others, and advising them to keep close to their Book which, although it did not contain precise and exact information as to details,

laid down with the utmost clearness the general principles which should guide them in cultivating new
trees. These men had not faith to believe that if the
right method were followed these young trees would
produce at last rich ripe fruit, and that a multitude of
people would, as of old, rejoice and find sustenance in
the flowers and fruit, and that the blessings of the old
tree would thus be indefinitely extended.

In "Quakerism Past and Present" J. S. Rowntree
forcibly described the evils arising from Birthright
Membership, and it was considered by some of the
most able and pious members of Dissenting Churches,
who had the most kindly feelings towards the Society
of Friends, that he had under-stated these evils, and
that this single matter of Birthright Membership was
sufficient in itself to account for the vast decline in
numbers of the Society in proportion to the increase
of the population. The Dissenting Churches of the
Commonwealth, although they had had their times of
depression, had not only maintained their increase
with the population, but had vastly increased their
numbers relatively to it. They considered that many
of the things which J. S. Rowntree considered *causes*,
were only the necessary *effects* of this one thing, and
that our eyes were blinded by the institution itself, or
that wê should long ago have condemned it as contrary to the principles of the New Testament which we
profess, and to right reason; and some of them have
declared that on similar arrangements as to Membership, their societies *could not exist and flourish* for many
years. A system of hereditary Membership would
necessarily vitiate the choice of Church officers, and
the healthy growth of the Society would be interfered
with, and a crop of evils and abuses would be gradually developed.

J. S. Rowntree's article in the *Quarterly Examiner*
practically tells us that his first thoughts were NOT

the best, and that in the matter of Membership the
Society has only to go on in a somewhat similar
groove; and he attacks the views of those among us
who have lately advocated what, we venture to think,
are more Scriptural and rational views of Membership
in a Christian Church.

One of the peculiarities of the Article is that he
gathers together all which has been said by those
whose views he wishes to refute, and *re-states* them.
The effect of this is to separate his adversaries' arguments and proposals from their natural connection, and,
like a skilful general, to attempt to defeat them in
detail.

He attempts to prove that of all Christian Churches
the mediæval Society of Friends, the Church of England, and the Church of Rome, have seized the true
idea of Membership in the visible Church of Christ,
excluding the more vigorous Protestant Churches in
this country, on the Continent, and especially in the
United States of America, who, in his opinion, have
developed false ideas as to Membership.

But not only does the writer inform us that he considers the reasons now thrown before us sufficient to
alter his own published opinions addressed to the
Christian world outside our Society as to the detri-
mental influence of Birthright Membership, but *"conclusive" against an attempt to substitute a better system.*
He presses upon our notice the fact that " two great
sections of the Christian Church," viz. the Roman
Catholic and the Church of England (see page 258)
" unite with Friends " in admitting infants into Church
Membership. He appears to consider, because the
greater part of the Christian world take these views,
that in some way this furnishes presumptive proof of their
correctness. Ought not this to be a strong inducement
to the Society of Friends to re-examine our position,
and to inquire whether the corruption and failing

strength of the Church of Rome and the Church of England, our own decline in numbers, and the small direct service we have rendered to the spread of Christianity, may not be contrasted with the work of the Protestant Dissenting Churches, who have had no small part in the great revival of Spiritual Religion during the last century ? It would be also profitable for us to consider if a sound system of Christian Membership has not had something to do with the force, energy, and enduring nature of the work in times past, and also whether the diffusion in later times, of less stringent ideas as to Christian Membership, such as those now advocated by J. S. R., has not had something to do with the present prevalence among these Churches of less ardour and devotion in the diffusion of the blessings of the Christian Religion.

We must first notice the allusion in this article to the fact that the controversy is not a new one, and that this was one of the difficulties of the Early Christian Churches that the question they debated was really the terms of Christian Association, or, as it is euphoniously termed in the article, " a difference of view between the advocates of a *restricted* and a *comprehensive* Membership." This allusion to the question as one which has remained unsettled for 1500 years would necessarily tend to make our Body hopeless of coming to a right decision—a state of mind eminently favourable for the question of Membership among us remaining untouched, unless we have the courage to go a little father and inquire, first, Why did this difficulty arise in the early Christian Church ? and secondly, Did the settlement of the question by what is termed the establishment of " a comprehensive Membership " tend to the maintenance of the original purity and efficiency of the visible Church, as an instrument both for the propagation of the Gospel, and for the training of its members and the children of its members in

Scriptural truth, and in a spiritual apprehension of the cardinal principles of the Gospel of Christ?

If we can answer these questions we shall be in a better position for judging whether our sympathies as a Protestant Church ought to be "alternately enlisted" first on one side and then on the other. Not only is this chapter in the History of the Church well worthy to be remembered, but we venture to think that the answers to these two questions will show that the introduction of this "Comprehensive Membership," or, in other words, of Infant Baptism, was the first step which tended to make the Kingdom of Christ a kingdom of this world, and paved the way for the great apostacy from the simplicity of the Gospel of Christ.

The celebrated Claudius Salmasius, of the University of Leyden, gives us the following information: " In the first two centuries after the birth of Christ, no one received baptism except those who were instructed in the faith and doctrine of Christ, and who were able to testify that they believed, in conformity with the words 'Whosoever believeth and is baptised,' &c. Therefore the first thing was to *believe*, and from this the order of the Catechumens arose in the Church. The custom was also firmly held as a perpetual one, that *after* baptism the Lord's supper should be given. After this the opinion gained ground that *only those who were baptised could be saved.* From this arose the custom of baptising infants at birth, and because they gave the Lord's supper to adult catechumens, after Infant Baptism was introduced, the Lord's supper was also administered to Infants."

Neander also distinctly tells us that Baptism, in the early Christian Church, was not originally applied to any but *adults*; because baptism and the possession of faith were strictly connected (Neander's History, Bohn's Standard Library, vol. iv. page 429, and vol. i. page 430), and also that "there does not appear to be *any* *reason for deriving Infant Baptism from an Apostolical Institution.*"*

Then came in the doctrine which condemned all men to perdition for the sin of Adam, and its logical sequence issued in the doctrine of the "damnation of unbaptised infants," and in consequence the extreme anxiety of Christian parents to have their offspring baptised, and thus the idea of a certain magical efficacy of baptism and the Lord's supper which were conceived to convey Grace to the recipient crept in. Then followed a view of the importance of a clear line of Apostolic Succession to convey, by bodily and visible means, this inherent efficacy.

We can readily see that the Baptism of the newly-born infants of Christian parents did away with the original *idea* and *intention*, and the *practical action* of the early Christian Church which was consequent upon this idea, viz. that a man or woman was first to be *convinced* by the preaching and teaching of Christianity of its *truth*. This led to the practice of handing over the converts to "Catechists." This was no distinct office in the early Church, but some persons who, it might be, had distinguished themselves among the Church readers of the New Testament Scriptures; and "able and learned laymen" were selected, *e.g.*, at Alexandria they were required to be "men of liberal education," who were able to satisfy the doubts and

---

* See also the First Apology of Justin Martyr, who is considered to have lived about the year A. D. 114, pages 59, 60 and 63, Ante-Nicene Library : " Since at our birth we were born without our own knowledge or choice, in order that we may not remain the children of necessity and ignorance, but may become the *children of choice* and knowledge, and may obtain in the Water of Baptism the remission of sins," &c. He says, page 59, that for Baptism "we have received *this reason* from the Apostles." And page 63 : "after we have thus washed him who has been *convinced* and *assented to our teaching.*"

objections of heathen, and meet them on their own ground. (See Neander, vol. i. 423.)

We believe that there is no evidence whatever that the children of Christian parents, except when their parents were able and willing to teach them the truths of Christianity, were in any case exempted from this teaching. In a word, some *knowledge of what Christianity* is, was found needful before any person could put faith in Christ, and resolve to "do the things which He says." And is it not equally needful now?

In the last year of the second century, Tertullian was a zealous opposer of Infant Baptism,* which is a sufficient proof, in the opinion of Neander, that the practice was not of apostolical institution, and that (to use J. S. R.'s words) a "Comprehensive Membership" was not the original Membership of the Church of Christ. Now what was the necessary effect of this universal prevalence of Infant Baptism at the time of Augustine and Donatus? It was this: Christianity became the inheritance of a particular division of mankind, viz., those who were fortunate enough to have Christian parents; and the idea of proclaiming the State a *Christian* State clearly arose from this—How great would be the gain of Christianity if we could baptise ALL the children who were born. Then the Church and State would be identical, and no further persecution could arise from pagan governors. Now, Donatus contended that " Church and State should be kept wholly distinct from each other," and the Bishop Donatus repelled the advances of the Imperial officer with the remark " What has the Emperor to do with

---

* With regard to young children Tertullian says " The Lord does indeed say ' Forbid them not to come unto me.' Let them ' come,' then, while they are growing up. Let them ' come' while they are learning—while they are being taught *whither* to ' come.' Let them become Christians when they have become able to *know* *Christ*."

the Church?"* (Neander, vol. iii. page 276). Again, the
Donatists maintained that the Church "should cast out
from its body those who were known by open and
manifest sins to be unworthy Members" (Neander, vol. iii.
page 291). They asked "Did the Apostles ever persecute
any one?" The Donatists urged, in reply to their adversaries who were contending for the retention of open
sinners in the Church, and for the *offices* of the Church
sanctifying the man, and not the man the office, that
"the field" in the parable quoted by J. S. Rowntree
"is the *world*" and not the Church; that the application of the parable of the net, proved that, in the
visible Church, the mixing in of secret sinners was inevitable—the object and construction of the net not
being to catch bad fish but good; that a complete separation was impossible, but what they demanded was
the "exclusion of persons manifestly vicious," from the
Society of believers. We may remark that the parable
of the field has been interpreted by the advocates of
the connection of the Church with the State in the
sense in which our friend J. S. R. interprets it, and by
all the advocates of the separation of Church and
State—by the early Independents, Baptists, and the
early Friends, in the same sense as the Donatists, and
they have all dwelt upon the interpretation of our Lord
as above quoted, setting aside all other human interpretation; and they come to the decision that "the
FIELD is the WORLD." We may reasonably be sus-
picious of the interpretation of this and similar texts
by the clergy of the Church of England, who have
been pledged, both by their solemn promises and by
the fact that the whole revenues of the State Church
hang upon this acceptance of the idea of a State Church

---

* He charged the Donatist Churches to receive none of the
Emperor's money. The Donatist Bishops also testified that the corruption of the Church had originated in the confusion of the Church
and State.

embracing a whole country, and on their receiving as Members of the Church, on principle, vicious as well as truly Christian persons.

Such were the principles of the Donatists, who appealed to numerous passages of Scripture to show that a Catholic Church corrupted by the *introduction* on principle and the *retention of unworthy Members,* was like those who bowed the knee to Baal; and the little band who held to the principles of the Apostles might, after all, be the real, visible Church, and be owned by Christ at his coming.

Surely our Religious Society ought not to be in *doubt* as to which principles it can, on the whole, accept. Surely the student of the facts of this controversy will not, if he has rightly understood and accepted our religious principles, indulge in that wavering disposition of mind, which our friend J. S. R. describes! Great principles were indeed involved; but we venture to hope that, after this necessarily imperfect statement of them, no Member of our Society will fail to see that those of the " Catholic Church " led to the enormous corruptions of Rome ; and that the same ideas in the Church of England, at the present time, are leavening this country with precisely the same principles, and that they are eating like a canker into the vitals of the English Church ; and what the reaping will be of such a sowing no one can predict. On the other hand, the principles of the Donatists, in the main, were principles of the Protestant Dissenters (and of the ancient Society of Friends), and were again developed by the Reformation, and thus the vital truths they contended for were not destined by Divine Providence to be lost.

This is the origin of the Infant Membership of the Church of England. If the Church was to be co-extensive with the State, it was necessary that every infant born within the State should be " christened :"

that is, *made a little Christian.*   J. S. Rowntree
appears to accept the explanation of certain Church of
England clergymen of ultra-liberal views, who have
kicked against the pricks of the clear and definite
doctrine of the Prayer Book, and therefore endeavour
so to interpret it as to make us believe that "the
Church" simply means to declare, *by means of Baptism,* that the infant is a participator in the salvation
which is by Christ, in the sense that, "He died for
all," is "the Saviour of all men," &c. &c.

This, we submit, is quite inconsistent with the facts
of the case. The Church of England maintains that,
by the rite of initiation into "the Church," the infant
becomes really "a Member of Christ, a child of God,
and an inheritor of the kingdom of Heaven." In the
27th Article of the Church of England it is distinctly
stated that Baptism is "a mark *of difference* whereby
Christian men are *discerned from others* that be NOT
christened."   In the "ministration of private Baptism" it is distinctly stated, that God (after Baptism)
has "regenerated this infant by His Holy Spirit,
and received him for His *own child by adoption,* and
incorporated him into His Holy Church," &c.

Now does it not appear, from these quotations, that
the Church of England idea of Membership in no way
agrees with those of our own Society, respecting outward Membership in the Church of Christ ? Do we
believe that there is only *one* visible Church of Christ ?
Do we believe that there is no salvation without an
outward connection with that, or any other Church ;
or that unconscious infants are "regenerated by the
Holy Spirit, and incorporated into God's Holy Church,"
either by Baptism, or enrolling their names on our
Meeting books ? If not, there is no real identity, or
even similarity, between our views of Membership and
those of the Church of England. This is still more
evident when we consider the rite of Confirmation

alluded to by J. S. Rowntree. By this ordinance, those who have arrived at "years of discretion," "ratify and confirm what their Godfathers and Godmothers promised for them," and the Bishop prays thus : —" Almighty and Everlasting God, Who has vouchsafed to regenerate these Thy servants by water and the Holy Ghost, and hast *forgiven them all their sins,* &c. (the qualification for Confirmation being, that the "child shall be able to say the Creed, and the Lord's Prayer, the Ten Commandments, and the Catechism.") In a word, the two Churches do not mean the same thing, by the two initiations into Membership, viz. Baptism, and the entry of an Infant upon the Register of Members of the Society of Friends.*

At the very point, however, where the example of the Church of England might suggest to an advocate of Birthright Membership a compromise, between those among us who object to Birthright Membership, and those who approve it, J. S. Rowntree sees the probability of our doing great injury by putting any questions to our young people when they arrive at years of understanding, even by their own consent ; and asking them, after the custom of the Church of England, whether they are prepared to "ratify and confirm" their Membership. † He appears

---

* It may also be remarked that in the United States the Anglican Church makes her *regular Communicants only,* Members.

† The writer of this article enjoyed, for some years, daily intercourse with our late dear friend William Tanner, and for many years had great opportunities of knowing his views on this subject, and believes that his objection was to the substitution of some Membership more objectionable than Birthright Membership. His opinion, at one time of his life, agreed substantially with our own, that, although the abolition of Birthright Membership ought to be steadily contemplated, it was "not the *first step that ought to be taken.*" This view he has repeatedly expressed to the writer, and we believe that his objection lay to "*calling upon* young persons, at a given age, to make a request to be considered Members," and to be

to consider that all *attenders* of our Meetings should be deemed Members, and be subjected to the operation of the discipline.* In his opinion, some pastoral visits should be paid to the children of our Members, on their arriving at their majority ; but what the officers of the Church should say is not indicated, although what they should *not* say is clearly specified.

Any such question as this, in his view, is unadvisable : " Art thou at peace with God through Jesus Christ; and is thy judgment satisfied to remain in communion with those among whom thou hast been born ?" (See page 264.) Any such questions might be fraught with serious consequences to the susceptible minds of the young, and therefore we are to choose the only alternative in his opinion, to continue to accept these persons as Members, and subject them to the operation of the discipline, *without the slightest volition on their part* on their coming to years of understanding! We agree with him in thinking such questions quite uncalled for and unnecessary, but do not accept the alternative.

---

striking them off our books if they did not make such application ; and he has often heard him use the expression that " such a sieve would let go much of the wheat, and retain much of the chaff," which evidently applies to a *demand.*

* See page 272.

CHAPTER II.

On the two great questions involved by Membership in any Church —Some Remarks on our Present Membership.

THERE has existed for some years, in the Church of England, a great agitation against subscription to Creeds and Articles, which has not been without its effect in other societies. This agitation is levelled against the means by which the Founders of this Church hoped to have secured a Christian Ministry, and which has proved abortive from the circumstance that the pious laity are shut out from the privilege of administering their own affairs and choosing their own ministers. The party, now called the Broad Church party, pursue the dream of a comprehension of all forms of belief in a National Church, with the object of retaining the funds of the State Church. We do not speak under the term of the Broad Church party of the followers of Whately, of Copleston, of Arnold, and of Hare, but of the party who would *now* admit, into the ministry of the Church of England, persons who do not believe in Christ, in *the sense in which the Apostles believed* in Him. They now ask for liberty to dissent from the opinions of the Apostles and Evangelists on the cardinal doctrines of the Gospel, such as justification by faith. They discredit the miraculous element of the New Testament, and, in truth, do not agree with the Apostle Paul when he tells the Corinthians that " if Christ be not raised " our " faith is *vain*," we " are yet in our sins." They see, however, great value in the bright moral lessons of Christianity, and they accept that only as religious truth which commends itself to what they term the " Verifying Faculty ;" and, having cut themselves adrift from the moorings of "the

c

Apostles' Teaching and Fellowship," Acts ii. ver. 42,
they approve of the reception by the Christian Church
of all shades of opinion, from Unitarianism to Deism,
and from Deism to Pantheism. We do not believe
for a moment, that our friend J. S. Rowntree would
approve the admission of persons to our membership
who do not accept the plain New Testament representation of what Christianity is ; but we say that the
proposal he has made to render indefinite the line
between Attenders and Members,* and to continue the
present system of Birthright Membership would inevitably *admit,* on principle, persons (such as the
founders of the Church of England intended to
exclude), both to membership and to all the offices of
the Society, including the Christian ministry, on one
simple condition, viz. that they are of ordinarily moral
and irreproachable lives. He is brought evidently to
this conclusion by his dread that the imposition of
some Creed, or Shibboleth (see page 266, line 1), either
written or spoken, would be necessary if Birthright
Membership were abolished. This brings us to the
point that at the threshold of the subject of Membership in any Church there are two questions, which
must be plainly answered before we can enter upon
the consideration of any collateral matters. Granting
that there are to be outward societies of men, called
Churches, the first question is : Is it necessary, or is it
not, that they should believe in Christ, in any sense
which corresponds to the New Testament definition of
the word Christian, Believer, Follower, or Disciple of
Christ ? This has nothing whatever to do with the
question respecting the imposition of Creeds, Articles,

---

*We do not see the slightest difficulty in the class of attenders
of our meetings becoming twice as numerous as at present, and it only
appears a difficulty from the point of view of Birthright Membership. The distinction has existed from the earliest ages of the Church.

and Subscriptions, and attempts "to gauge spiritual experience." We fully agree with J. S. Rowntree, that membership in the Society of Friends, or in any Church, should be based, to a considerable extent, upon agreement in practice, and particularly in practical methods of unitedly labouring in the cause of Christ, and not upon minute questions as to doctrine or creed. But we maintain that an answer to our first question is inevitable. If we answer that it is *not* necessary that a member should believe in Christ, or be a disciple of Christ, in the plain and ordinary New Testament sense, we are involved in the absurdity of asserting that the great Founder of the outward and visible Church, and His Apostles, admitted, *on principle*, persons who were enemies to Christ and his Gospel, and persons who were perfectly lukewarm and indifferent. That Christ himself admitted Judas ; that the Laodiceans were lukewarm and indifferent; that there were persons among the Church of Corinth who did not believe in the Resurrection, has nothing to do with the question we are now dealing with. Even our friend J. S. R., would not contend that Judas was a traitor when our Lord admitted him ; or that the Laodiceans were lukewarm and indifferent when they *first* became members ; or that disbelievers in the Resurrection were admitted, *as such*, into the Church of Corinth. If then we say that those who profess to believe in Christ, *i.e.* Christians, alone are eligible as members of any outward Society professing to be a Christian Church, are we necessarily involved in the dilemma of either approving Birthright Membership or of laying down a purely doctrinal basis for membership ?

We think that J. S. R. has, by an illustration of his own, shown that this need not be the case ; and yet that membership in the outward and visible Church, in the time of the Apostles, was never granted without an outward profession of faith in Christ. In the words

of the Apostle Paul : " If thou confess with thy mouth
the Lord Jesus, and believe in thy heart that God
raised Him from the dead, thou shalt be saved;" and
the burden of proof rests upon those who deny that
any other class of persons, but those who were such,
were received into outward fellowship.   He remarks,
very truly, that the early Christian Church (page 273)
" opened its arms to *converts in the first stages of
Christian experience."* *

We are not aware that it has ever been proposed,
by the advocates of any more scriptural and rational
system of membership in our Society, that any
other course should be followed ; and, curiously
enough, in J. S. R.'s own statement (page 254) of
their views, *they are not represented as demanding
a more narrow basis than the early Church of the New
Testament.*   The instance adduced in proof of the
remark quoted above, is that of the Ethiopian Eunuch,
(Acts viii. 37), and we venture to think that it proves
a great deal *more* than he intends it to prove.

The Eunuch's question to Philip was, "See, here is
water, what doth hinder me to be baptised ?" (*i.e.*
received by an outward sign that he was washed,
cleansed, sanctified in the name of the Lord Jesus,
and by the Spirit of our God, as a *fit* person to be a
member of ANY outward Christian Society.)

What is Philip's reply?   " If thou *believest with all
thine heart* thou mayest."   He puts the responsibility
before God upon the conscience of the supposed convert, and the convert answers, " I believe that Jesus

---

* Tertullian, in the year A.D. 207 to 217, remarks pithily upon
this : "If Philip so easily baptised the Chamberlain, let us reflect
that a manifest and conspicuous evidence that the Lord deemed him
worthy was interposed." (252 vol. i., Works Ante-Nicene Library.)
This illustrates how there was a tendency in the Church then to
press for the easy admission of unsuitable candidates, which he very
rightly rebukes.

Christ is *the* Son of God;" and Philip, considering this doubtless as a credible profession of faith, and from the heart, baptised him.

We conclude that no person who ever read this doubted that we have here the reception of a person into the Visible Church, and that we have here the apostolic condition of membership.

Is this "unfavourable to the proposal of making membership dependent on *personal application* ?"— see p. 271 (where it is said, without attempt at proof, that the *experience of various Churches* is NOT in *favour* of this practice.) Was this submission to a 'creed verbal or written' (see p. 266) an attempt by the evangelist Philip to "gauge," to "subject to human scrutiny," the spiritual life of his convert? Was this "a formal confession of faith?" (see pp. 263, 264) and would the omission of the enquiry of Philip have been "eminently successful in stamping the sense of personal responsibility" on the Ethiopian? which is claimed by J. S. R. as a feature of our present system of membership.

Is it not obvious that Philip does not assume any knowledge of the exact state of the man's heart, but that he rests the responsibility of the convert's profession upon the man himself? It was no question of whether Philip had "spiritual and mental affinities" with the person, nor of the convert's "powers of expression," which it appears now play so large a part in influencing Committees for the reception of members among us (p. 265); nor of the "pronunciation of theological formulas"; or shibboleths (see p. 266); nor of Philip's fitness to constitute himself a "judge of the spiritual condition" (p. 265) of the said convert; but the sole question was, *had he the belief with all the heart,* which the Eunuch immediately expressed in the earnest words, "I believe that Jesus Christ is *the* Son of God"? Ages of experience in the Church

Universal, and a century and a half of experience in our own, has proved by sad experience, that a perfectly moral and irreproachable walk in life does not necessarily evince heartfelt faith in Christ, the Son of God.

The character of our sins and temptations depends upon our education and position. There is *no Christian* love without living faith. It is "faith working by love" which makes a Christian. Faith without love is like a flower which does not come to perfection. The Society of Friends would, in our opinion, have been spared many sorrowful episodes in its history, and peculiar difficulties, especially in dealing with young people—such, for instance, as it has experienced at Manchester—had it from its origin on principle uniformly asked the question which Philip asked the Ethiopian, of all applicants for membership. Had this been so, we think that Birthright Membership would never have been instituted.

Here we must object to the representation which is given (see p. 254) of the views of those who consider that a public profession of faith in Christ, and a *voluntary* personal application should precede membership in an outward Church. They consider, it is stated, that an outward or visible Church is "a company of Christian people, who should *be made to correspond* in their membership with that spiritual Body of which the Lord Jesus Christ is the living Head," and that the Society of Friends, as a Church, is "*bound to see* that its members *are* religious persons." This is, we venture to think, NOT what they say; they do not believe that any human arrangements whatever will succeed in "*making*" a perfectly pure Church or Society; but what they say is, that human arrangements, which receive on principle into visible Churches (—the Divinely appointed instruments for the propagation of the Christian religion) persons who, upon J. S. Rowntree's own showing (we say it advisedly) may be the deadliest opponents of Christ's religion ; and who, with all the care which can be expended upon their religious education, to use J. S. R.'s words, "as years pass will depart farther and farther from the fold of Christ," and those, too, who become middle-aged men and women, "without having made a decided choice between allegiance to Christ or to the world."—They say that human arrangements which receive *such* persons into Christian communion, unsolicited by the persons themselves, and without even consulting them, frustrate the Divine intentions, and the objects of any human society called a Church. They say that though man cannot "*make*" a perfectly pure Church on earth, man can "*make*" an impure and unholy Church. "What communion hath light with darkness ? or he that believeth with an infidel?" asks the apostle Paul; and is the fact that such persons are now generally born of Christian parents in a Christian country a less reason for refusing to receive them into the Christian Church ?

There is, therefore, too much truth in the remark that the Christian army is paralysed in its movements by the constant pouring into its ranks, by a human arrangement, of those who are either not followers of the great Captain of their Salvation, or who have never asked for communion or membership.

Again, who could so define the duty of the Society of Friends, as a Church, that it is bound "to *see* that its members are religious persons "? How any Church can do this we cannot conceive. What *is* said is this —That the whole conception of the character and objects of the outward and visible Church implied by Birthright Membership, is erroneous and contrary to the great principles of Church Architecture laid down in the New Testament, when an arbitrary number of persons is separated from the great world (be they the

Society of Friends, or the inhabitants of a province or
of a kingdom) and all their newly-born infants are
made Members of *the*, or rather *a*, church. The
opponents of our present Membership say that the
outward and visible Church consists of persons
who are *voluntarily* induced, by the Holy Spirit, to
unite, on the basis—without any attempt to " gauge "
spiritual experience, or to " compare themselves among
themselves "—of a profession of Faith in Christ as the
Son of God, in a Society for their mutual encouragement to walk in this evil world as becometh the
Gospel of Christ, and for the great purposes of propagating this Gospel and building each other up in their
most holy faith. These persons are witnesses to the
world of the truth of the Christian religion, and fur-
nish to the world an outward evidence of the reality
of their conviction, by their joint action, and the sacrifices of time, money, and reputation which they make
unitedly for the propagation of their religion. If we
rob this action of its spontaneous character—by reck-
oning persons to be what they are not, or by "asking"
them to become what they have no heart to become—
the Church is shorn of all its strength. It is true that
men may profess what is untrue, and enter the Church
as hypocrites—or they may become hypocrites after
they have entered—but those who are *not* Christians
are not devoid either of conscience or of honour, and
when a Church keeps true to its Divine objects there
is little to attract the worldly-minded.*

---

* We do desire to attract the world to hear the preaching of the
Gospel. Hence the very great importance of drawing the distinction between Attenders at a place of worship and professed Christians. It was the object of our Blessed Lord to attract as many as
possible to hear. He accommodated his movements to this end :
preached on the mountain, on the steps of the Temple, in the boat,
&c. &c. ; but He *chose* twelve, commissioned the seventy, bid the
wavering one to "*follow me*," and let the dead bury their dead,
&c. &c.

On the one hand we have the *systematic reception* of all who are *born within a given circle*; if we receive all the World so born we must receive on principle all the hypocrites, &c. &c. in that particular section of it, into the bosom of the Church. On the other, we receive a very few persons who succeed in deceiving us. It is precisely like a shopkeeper who receives young men with high professions and a good character, and because one here and there turns out a thief and robs the till, he is counselled not to believe any longer in human nature, but to receive young men to attend his counter who make "*no profession*" of being honest, and of having a good character, and a desire to serve him faithfully. We can conceive this *defended in theory*, but would it answer in practice? This brings us to the second question.

It is obvious that any particular Church or Society of persons, such as have been described, have the power of laying down certain principles and rules for their guidance as an outward Society. How can any walk together unless they be agreed?

Our discipline, for instance, depends for its sanction entirely on the words of our Lord, "If thy brother trespass against thee, tell him his fault between thee and him alone; if he shall hear thee, thou hast gained thy brother," &c. ; and *in the last resort* we are to "tell it to the Church." Our peculiar views respecting War, Oaths, the Ministry of the Gospel, &c., depend again on the New Testament for their authority. What arrangements the Society or Church thinks fit to make respecting pastoral care over its members, the visitation of the sick, widows, and fatherless, and the poor in their affliction; the performance by deputy of what cannot possibly be done by every member of the flock; the methods to be taken for preaching the Gospel to the world; for providing sound Scriptural instruction for the children of mem-

bers *; are all matters of agreement, respecting which
the importance of a mutual understanding between a
Church and a Christian joining that Church cannot be
denied. We receive general instruction on these matters in the New Testament, and although certain great
principles are there laid down, still these are subjects
on which Christian men and women may reasonably
differ in opinion. In every human institution for real
work, to ensure harmonious working, a distinct *agreement* on the part of the person proposing to join such
a Society, is found to ensure both harmony and
vigorous co-operation among the members in carrying
out the great ends of any Institution. Hence the
absolute necessity of some such agreement as to the
outward constitution of a Church. It may be by
active labour, or by sympathy and encouragement,
or the dedication of worldly goods to the service;
but still, Christians, while united by faith to their one
living Head, are compelled (like citizens of the world),
to secure these great ends by uniting in various Societies
or Churches. Therefore there is a clear ground for the
existence of the Society of Friends, the Baptist, Independent, Methodist, and Presbyterian Societies, &c.
&c.† Freedom of conscience is secured by our perfect
liberty to unite with one or other of these Societies.
The principle of welcoming a man, who is known
to be united by faith to our common Lord, and
of holding religious communion with Him—in some
cases even admitting him to preach and pray in their
assemblies, without asking him to *unite in their
work or Society*—is increasingly acted upon, and is, we

---

* Of which our public schools are nearly the only instance in our
Body, and appear positively to comprise all the religious care they
receive.

† The Church of England *contains* a Church, but is not strictly
speaking a Church, having no power of self-government.

think, a sound and most important principle, which
will bear the closest scrutiny, and is calculated to
produce the most blessed fruits. We may remark,
too, in passing, that the reason why the Plymouth
Brethren have been so grievously divided, is not, as
J. S. R. conceives, because they draw a strong, and,
perhaps exaggerated, line of demarcation between believers and unbelievers, but because they try to *unite
together simply on the ground* of the Communion of
believers; recognising. the New Testament as their
written law, and feeling a strong objection to laying
down any further basis for their action as a Society.
There is no agreement as a Church, that such and such
New Testament principles lead them to such and such
provisions as to certain practical methods of carrying
out the great ends of an outward church. Therefore
the appeal is not to a recognised basis of procedure in
matters of Discipline and Church Government, but
directly to the New Testament on each occasion; and
we have the authority of members of that community for
saying that *this*, and other similar defects in their
arrangements, have greatly conduced to their lamen-
table divisions.* They are principally composed of

---

* The following has been received from our friend John Eliot
Howard, of Tottenham, who we need hardly remark is an eminent
member of the more liberal section of the Churches of the Plymouth
Brethren :—

"I have carefully examined the statements you have laid before
me ; and remark, in the first place, that the strictures of J. S.
Rowntree do not appear to me founded on any clear acquaintance
with facts. I cannot perceive that 'the attempt to draw a strong
line of demarcation between believers and others' had anything
whatever to do with the internal dissensions of the 'Brethren.'
In my private opinion they were, in the origin, too lax in this
respect ; so that individuals, such as Professor Newman, were
accredited, more on the ground of professed zeal and self-denial, than
of *any* confession of faith, except that which is *implied* in the
participation in the Lord's Supper. The dissensions that have
unhappily arisen commenced amongst the leaders—men generally

persons who are dissatisfied with other Churches. Some
disapprove of all organised societies, some are Calvinists
of the strictest school, some are Arminians like ourselves. It can readily be conceived that, among men
who are not united on more than one point (a union,
sufficient indeed for the Saints in Light, but quite
insufficient for men with human frailties), the want of
this clear understanding, which worldly men, in their
greater wisdom, first secure from the members of their
societies, is a great loss. They cannot appeal to any
rules, &c., accepted by all who enter the Society.
It is thus that the churches of the Plymouth Brethren
necessarily present a spectacle which is a living pro-
test against the principles which J. S. Rowntree endeavours to commend to our notice, when he suggests
that all attenders be deemed members, even without
the basis of agreement among the Plymouth Brethren.
With regard to the practice of the Methodists, Con-
gregationalists, and Baptists, J. S. Rowntree seems
to be under the impression that they require a subscription to doctrinal articles before a person is received
a member. We append a note received by the author
from E. B. Underhill, LL.D., the Secretary of the
Baptist Missionary Society and who is chosen Presi-
dent of the Baptist Union for the coming year; and
from James H. Rigg, of the Training College for
Teachers, and member of the Wesleyan Conference

---

of rather High Church views of ecclesiastical authority, and with
a *full* share, it may be, of human infirmity. They would not bear
with each other; and though their points of difference may be
viewed in different lights, I conceive that they would generally be
unintelligible to ordinary Christians. I do not by this deny their
importance, but wish it clearly to be understood that they do not
at all justify Mr. Rowntree's remarks. Such leaders, unless they
had more grace, must always have found grounds of dissension, and
were sure to rend the flock asunder."

and of the London School Board, which shews this is not the case.*

---

* *Extracts from a letter from E. B. Underhill, LL.D., Secretary of the Baptist Missionary Society, Editor of the Hansard Knollys Society's publications, &c. &c.* :—

"Baptist Mission House, 17th Nov., 1872.

"In answering your questions, I can speak from experience as to the practice of Baptist Churches in receiving members. There is no uniform mode among us. But *I never heard* of any church requiring a candidate to receive or subscribe to a creed. The one object sought is some satisfactory evidence that the candidate has been truly converted to God, that his life has undergone the great change signified by the word 'regeneration.' In doing this the methods vary."

Dr. Underhill goes on to describe the methods. The applicant in all cases first sees the pastor; afterwards the church generally appoints two or three members to visit the applicant; and the only inquiries addressed to the applicant are whether he believes in the main doctrines of the Gospel. "No creed or formulary is adduced or produced, nor is the candidate required to express his assent to any creed. I think I may positively say that this practice. is universal in every Baptist church. Independent churches act in the same way; but it is understood that they are not quite as rigid as Baptist churches in their requirements."

"The Methodists, I believe, require of any person joining their classes a single profession of a desire to save their souls. If they attend regularly, and satisfy their leader of their sincerity, they are soon admitted to the communion. But the spirit of the class system is such that any careless or wicked person is soon eliminated from the class, and his standing in the Society comes to an end."

Extract from a letter received from James H. Rigg, Principal of the Wesleyan Training College (for School Teachers), Member of the London School Board, Author of "Essays for the Times," &c.

"Wesleyan Training College, S.W.,
"13th Jan., 1873.

"In answer to your inquiry, I will quote from our 'Rules of Society.'. "There is only one condition previously required of those who desire admission into these societies, viz., 'a desire to flee from

We would, therefore, ask:—Though our religious Society has escaped the error of the Plymouth Brethren, of not laying down a definite basis of agreement as to the principles and rules on which its operations are to be conducted, does it not fall into an equally grave error ? In the first place it accepts persons and places them under the operation of these rules, who may not be Christians at all, and therefore have no interest whatever in the working of the Society, unless it be to work it so as, either consciously or unconsciously, to impede the objects of the Great Head of the Church, such as the evangelisation of the world, the comfort and consolation, and communion of the church members, &c. ; and, in the second place, it applies the discipline and urges the rules and objects of the Society upon young people who have never accepted them, and they are treated as necessarily approving these things, (because forsooth, they are good and excellent) when they have never so approved them. Or, in the third place, it places them in such a position that, just at the most critical and most sensitive portion of their religious life, they must either acquiesce in what they

---

the wrath to come, and to be saved from their sins.' But wherever this is fixed in the soul it will be shown by its fruits," &c.

"Such a society is no other than a company of men having the form and seeking the power of godliness; united in order to pray together, to receive the word of exhortation, and to watch over one another in love, that they may help each other to work out their salvation. No member is ever required to make a profession of faith, public, or private, before the church, or to the class, or to the minister. The life and essence of our church organisation is *fellowship*. The man who is willing to become a *fellow*, to join actually in the fellowship, is received forthwith, and if he lives consistently is retained. The last thing Mr. Wesley would have consented to would have been to make any *creed* or *opinion* a condition of church fellowship with his societies." The partaking of the communion is among the Wesleyans practically essential to membership, and is equivalent to the profession of faith in Christ.

have never had submitted to their judgment, or separate themselves from their nearest and dearest friends. Suppose a young person has imbibed sceptical views and has the strength of mind not to be ashamed of his or her opinion, and even, to some extent, propagates it. He regards the interference of the Church as a piece of ecclesiastical tyranny, and says, " I am willing to be convinced, but you threaten me with a kind of social ban, a sentence of excommunication; and this is to me the worst argument in the world." His membership is his *birthright,* he is part of a respectable corporation, possessing large property and certain educational advantages. He has entered into no promises, he is under no obligations to the Society, he has not even had the opportunity of accepting or refusing any religious instruction from Ministers called to such work, and approved by the Church. He considers he is not bound in honour to make himself master of the opinions of the Church, propounded in the Book of Extracts. The necessary action of the Society, if it would vindicate its position as a Christian Church, is, to his mind (and who shall venture to say that it is not really so ?) an act of injustice. The origin of all this complication is obviously Birthright Membership *alone.* Reverse the picture, he is merely a child of a member of the Society. The Church has a mission to *him ;* it seeks to make him a Christian ; it sets apart and encourages certain of its members who have the gifts of the Holy Spirit for such service ; its message to him concerns the interests of his *immortal soul.* Our Society is not endeavouring to flatter him by putting him on trifling Church appointments and attempting to allure him *merely to join a Society ;* it does not cry to him helplessly, " How are our Meetings for Discipline to be kept up if *thou* dost not come to them ?" It entreats him to receive the message from Heaven which it bears ; its duty is " to give a reason " to every one who

asks " a reason" of our exalted hopes. The spirit of
opposition gives way before the meekness which in-
structs, and in such service a shower of Heavenly
gifts and graces descends upon weak, fallible men,
yielding themselves to be the organs of the Holy Spirit
for the conversion of the world. The surpassing glories
of the Person of Christ, the mystery of the Cross, the
reality of the New Creation, are exhibited by the
servants of Christ and of the Church, as men whose
office is to *persuade,* not to *enforce* or *command.*

Instead of our Ministers gathering congregations,
we have whipped-up—by means of applying the Discipline to persons to whom it does not properly apply—
congregations to our Ministers, and have not encouraged
our Ministers to seek fresh congregations; and many
a pious and learned man (in the best sense), who would
have secured a congregation of 500 or 1,000 persons,
has laboured in our Meetings for half a life-time, hardly
seeing the slightest fruit of his labours, and has
wondered why it is, and has put it down, in his deep
humility, to want of personal holiness ; when the fact
is that he has been preaching to persons who, as a congregation, do not seek his ministry from a desire to
be taught; to persons who, generally speaking, have
not been gathered by the " preaching of the Gospel,"
but on another principle. But we will take another
case, where the Society is dealing with a *worldly* young
man, and stands at the bar of public opinion. He is,
we will suppose, the son of some wealthy Friend,
and well educated, but has never made any profession
of belonging to the Society. He is known by them as
a gay young man, caring nothing for religion, although
he attends our Meetings. He falls into a snare and
his moral character is at stake. His family are valued
Members of our Body. His father rebukes him and for-
gives him, and his moral nature eventually re-asserts
its superiority. The matter, for the sake of the young

man, is a family secret. An Overseer hears of the case and does his duty faithfully. The young man is publicly disowned by a Christian Society to which he *never made the slightest pretence of belonging by any tie of conviction*, and the Society of Friends is the executioner of his public disgrace. His father, as a Minister in the Society, was bound by every consideration which can bind one of its officers, to carry out its discipline, and to denounce his son, did not the ties of nature prove themselves stronger than the system of Birthright Membership, which places every one, Father, Overseer, and young man in a false position. If the Overseer is lax, other denominations lift up their hands in astonishment and say—as the writer has heard said— " You have some excellent Christian people among you, but we cannot understand how you can consider *such* and *such* young people as *Members* ?"

Shall we blame the young man if he considers that he has suffered an injustice ? Will the carefully-worded and well-balanced statement of our friend, of the position the Society occupies towards him, avail J. S. R. when he speaks to those who are without ? Will they not answer him that the Society may tacitly take what position it will, but the question is, do the persons concerned *accept* its position, viz., that, because they have been *entered in infancy on its books,* therefore, unless they send in their resignation, they desire to belong to it, and are supposed willing substantially to approve the official exposition of the Rules, Doctrine and Practice of the Society ? We ask, do " those who seriously demur to this exposition," " naturally retire " from the community which issues it ? (v. page 262).

We never heard the subject put to our young people on attaining years of understanding, as J. S. R. in fact puts it—' If you do not substantially approve all which is contained in our Book of Discipline, we do not wish to retain you as Members.' We have never

D

heard the opinion expressed, either among young or old, that a Member of the Society of Friends is bound in honour to retire from the Society on any such grounds. Here is really the secret of the want of sympathy between the ideas of the older and younger Members. Our younger Members, who are religiously inclined, are engaged in labours which appear to them more important for the interests of the Christian religion than the work of the Society. They do not approve of many things in our Society. Our Church officers have never been obliged to seek to make use of them for the service of the Church. They have never been compelled to win the undecided and irreligious children of our Members, or to raise up congregations from the world.

Hence the unbending and rigid position of the Society! It is self-contained; it is recruited without thought or care; it has not to consider the *conditions* on which anxious and thoughtful young Christians will desire to become Members. It has so long lived on conditions different from those of a vigorous, missionary Church, that it shrinks and sees its doom forestalled in the abolition of Birthright Membership. Parents shrink lest their children should leave the Society; and they have more trust in *not challenging any attention to the views of the Society* than in any other system; and hope that their children, having obtained the distinction before the world, of being Members of a Christian Church without trouble on their part, or serious thoughtfulness on the part of their children, may afterwards become truly Christian young people. These youthful Christians only obtain a status and position after the qualification of many years of regular attendance at Meetings for Discipline, instead of being early and cordially welcomed, as they were in the early Society, and as they are in some other Churches, as the great means of their support and the perpetuation of their Christian principles.

To those who have closely watched the effects of our system, there is also a singular absence of complete confidence by the Church in our members, which leads to a barren appointment of Committees to confer and report, rather than to a *selection of persons* having Christian gifts and graces, and a real concern to strive to bring about the desired end. This is, we conceive, the direct result of an hereditary membership. There is too much disposition in our Body calmly to see the mill grind without asking, or even expecting, definite results; and to accept the regular working of so much machinery for a proof of religious prosperity, and it is obvious that this apathy exists because the Society is not obliged to depend upon its own exertions for existence. It is not sufficient to have "old men for counsel and young men for war." It is only "in the Lord" that either young or old can have "counsel or might." It is mainly by the recognition of Divine instruments, and by a spirit of hearty co-operation with them, and by liberal and self-denying support of such persons by Visible Churches, that the greatest triumphs of the Gospel have been obtained.

The Christian religion can never assert its force— under conditions such as these—in winning the masses of the population. If, as stated in the essay, "the data from which a right conclusion is to be deduced" in this matter are the "results of the various regulations in force in different branches of the Christian Church," who do not "run counter to the principles laid down by the Lord Jesus for the government of the Church," we may soon learn, and the writer has shown elsewhere, that the Churches who have been *the most successful* in propagating the Christian religion, have ALL a definite Membership of the character we have been speaking of, and not a Birthright Membership.

Our discipline—if it were applied to those persons only who are professed members of Christ's Church, and who accepted the regulations of the Society, modified as they would be by the necessities of the case—would be most salutary, and could not in any possible case, either be mis-represented, or, with the help of the Holy Spirit, ever misapplied. It would then apply only to persons who had *violated the conditions on which they became Members*, and much time which might be spent more profitably might be saved to the cause of Christ. It would be most useful in case of the Society being, in the providence of God, the means of any large ingathering. Is it too much to hope for that it will ever be thus used?

CHAPTER III.

On the Membership of the Early Society of Friends.

WE annex the following extract from J. S. Rowntree's Prize Essay, "Quakerism, Past and Present," written in 1859, which will shew his views at that period.

"The year 1737 is remarkable as being that in which "Membership" was first recognised by the Yearly Meeting. Previous to that period (as before observed) the only criterion for determining connection with the Society of Friends was habitual attendance at its religious meetings. Nor in times of persecution was any other required; but at the period we we have now reached, 'when the profession of a Friend no longer tested individual conviction, difficulty arose in determining the limits of the Society's responsibility for the exercise of its discipline and the proper relief of its poor," which induced the Yearly Meeting to issue the following minute : 'That all Friends shall be deemed Members of the Quarterly, Monthly, or Two-weeks' Meeting, within the compass of which they inhabited or dwelt the First-day of Fourth Month, 1737.' Many years elapsed before the consequences resulting from this enactment fully developed themselves. In some respects the evils that have arisen from it are more evident at the present time than had previously been the case; but we conceive, it might have been early discovered, that to make Membership in a Christian Church dependent on the accident of birth, was very much to abandon the New Testament idea of a Church. Instead of being a company of faithful men and women, united in religious fellowship, and possessing a strong bond of union in heartfelt allegiance to their common Lord, the Society of Friends increasingly assumed the character of a corporation, existing for ends partly religious, partly social, and partly civil; and containing a number of persons unconverted to God. From the children of Friends being registered as Members at the time of birth, and being esteemed such till their names are removed by death, disownment, or resignation, even should they give little or no evidence of the possession of personal piety, Membership has virtually become hereditary, having certain privileges contingent on its possession, and descends from father to son almost like other property. From this anomalous provision operating in conjunction with their marriage regulations, the Friends, as they have declined in numbers, have become increasingly bound together by family relationship ; and whilst the spirit of clan-ship has conferred some elements of strength, it has also favoured the growth of that exclusive feeling which is rarely absent from any association of men, in which Membership is principally obtained through hereditary descent. Such bodies, it is well known, look suspiciously on the infusion of new blood into their constitution, and a feeling of this character has had a powerful influence amongst the Friends during the last century in making them indifferent to the obtaining of proselytes.

"In the latter part of last century the difficulties that arose from 'meetings for discipline' being merely composed of a few *elder Friends** (sometimes possessing little qualification for the office, but that of age), induced *a change in their constitution*, and gradually the attendance of all 'Members' (*i.e.* the new 'Members' constituted by the definition of the Yearly Meeting—Birthright Members) was en-couraged. After this change, the weakness occasioned by the retention of numerous nominal adult 'Members,' having a right to assist in its Church government, and generally to influence the policy of the Body, became more apparent. The presence of children in disciplinary Meetings (as listeners merely) has been decidedly beneficial, and constitutes an important educational agency ; but we think that, had some arrangement existed by which young persons on attaining to years of maturity should make a simple profession of their faith,

---

* It was no strictly necessary result of the regulations of the Early Society that it so happened, since, originally, it accepted and made extensive use of the services of young and able men. The qualification for Members of the Meetings for Discipline was correct and Scriptural ; but the dread of any outward form or ceremony in the reception of Members of these Meetings, as the equivalent of Baptism, left the application of the definition of a properly qualified member to the " Elders," *i.e.* settled Ministers, and there-fore the great principles of the Early Friends respecting Church Membership did not form a basis of action in the Monthly Meetings, and were therefore gradually forgotten, because not embodied in a positive institution.

or renounce their 'Membership' in the Body, it would have operated as a powerful stimulus to serious parents, as well as to healthy congregations, in giving their children and young people that careful religious training which would be the most fitting preparation for such a profession. It would also have prevented or lessened the evils arising from the retention of merely nominal Members. The maxim, that 'what is easily obtained is lightly esteemed,' declares a true principle; and from 'Membership' being so indiscriminately granted to all the children of Friends, it is often regarded by them when rising into manhood or womanhood, in a false light; instead of being esteemed a privilege—as Membership with a Christian Church should ever be—it has been felt to be a burden, imposing restraints not demanded by their own consciences. Family ties, or other causes, often prevent such young people from separating the connection between themselves and the Society; the Church itself will not do it, unless some act penal under its discipline be committed; and so they remain, sometimes throughout a long lifetime (if we may accommodate Lord Macaulay's metaphor), 'Members of the Society'; 'but withered and distorted Members, adding no strength to the Body, and reproachfully pointed at by all who fear or envy the greatness' of Quakerism.

" When the regulations respecting Membership had existed thirty or forty years, a considerable body of persons grew up, attending Meetings for worship, and making more or less of profession with the Friends, but not in Membership.

"As this class was constantly recruited from parties who were disowned, but who retained some affection for their former principles or practices, by the children of such persons, and from other sources, it has increased to such an extent as now to constitute more than one quarter of all the worshippers in the Meeting-houses of Friends. How suitably to provide for the education, oversight, and marriage arrangements of this large body of persons, not considered as forming an integral part of the Society, but separated from it by an arbitrary and accidental line only, has been a source of continual difficulty; and by neglecting these duties, loss has been occasioned to the individuals themselves, and much weakness to the Society induced."

Thus wrote our friend in 1859. We would ask our readers candidly to consider what valid reasons have been given in the article published in the *Quarterly Examiner* of Fourth Month, 1872, for an entire change of view upon this important subject? The fact that an hereditary Society has no urgent need for recruiting its Members explains *why* so little care has been extended to "attenders;" and the want of a TRUE line of demarcation has rendered this " arbitrary and accidental " only.

We now propose to deal with that part of the article which treats of the nature of the Membership of the Society of Friends in 1672, and comparing it with that existing in 1872. This is a subject with which, from the foregoing quotation, it will be seen that our friend is intimately acquainted. He brings forward no new facts in the article of 1872. It is for him to explain why the facts now tell a tale they never seem to have suggested to his mind in 1859.

To enable our readers to understand this we append the statement contained at p. 253 of the article, thus summing up his conclusion :—

" Speaking generally, therefore, we think the statement that Birthright Membership is a modern institution is not sustained. From the rise of Friends the children of its members have always been deemed to belong to it. It is not necessary to pursue this historical enquiry further." (P. 253).

It will be obvious that the quotation from the prize essay is intended to give an historical explanation of the *gradual introduction* of a Birthright Membership. Again (p. 252) : " When we come to enquire what is the difference in the relation of the Society to the children of its members at the two periods, but *little change* is apparent." While in the prize essay J. S. R. endeavours to convince us that the facts show a *great change* took place.

Let our readers carefully read the following quotation from Barclay's " Apology" :—

" Those things which I, together *with my brethren,* do believe concerning the Church. .' . . To be a member of *a particular* Church of Christ, as this inward work is indispensably necessary, so is also the *outward profession of,* and belief in, Jesus Christ, and those holy truths delivered by his Spirit in the Scriptures, seeing the testimony of the Spirit recorded in the Scriptures, doth answer the testimony of the Spirit in the heart, even as *face answereth face in a glass.* Hence it follows that the inward work of holiness, and forsaking iniquity, is necessary in every respect to the being a member in the *Church of Christ.* . . . After that the princes of the earth came to take upon them that profession, and that it ceased to be a reproach to be a Christian, but rather became a means to preferment, men became such *by birth and education,* and not by conversion and renovation of spirit. . . . For, as to the nature and constitution of a Church (abstract from their disputes concerning its constant visibility, infallibility, and the primacy of the Church of Rome), the Protestants, as in practice so in principles, differ not from Papists ; for they engross within the compass of their Church *whole nations,* making their *infants members* of it, by sprinkling a little water on them ; so that there is none so wicked or profane who is not a fellow-member; no *evidence* of holiness being *required* to constitute a member of the Church. . . . But this inward call, power, and virtue of the Spirit of God is necessary to make a man a Christian, as we have abundantly proved before in the Second Proposition, according to these Scriptures, ' He that hath not the Spirit of Christ is none of his.' ' As many as are led by the Spirit of God are the sons of God.' . . . For Jesus Christ, as He regardeth not any distinct particular family or nation in the gathering of his children, but only such as are joined to and leavened with his own *pure and righteous* seed ; so neither regards He a bare outward succession, where his pure, immaculate, and righteous life is wanting, for that were all one. He took not the nations into the *new covenant,* that He might suffer them to fall into the old errors of the Jews, or to approve them in their errors, but that He might gather unto Himself a pure people out of the earth. Now was this the great error of the Jews, to think they were the Church and people of God, because they could derive their *outward succession* from Abraham ; whereby they reckoned themselves the *children of God,* as being the *offspring of Abraham,* who was the *Father of the Faithful.* But how severely doth the Scripture rebuke this vain and frivolous pretence! Telling them 'that God is able of the stones to raise children unto Abraham,' and that not the *outward 'seed'* but those that are found in the '*faith*' of Abraham, are the true 'children of faithful Abraham.' Far less, then, can this pretence hold among Christians, seeing Christ rejects all outward affinity of that kind. 'These,' saith He, 'are my mother, brethren and sisters, who do the will of my Father which is in heaven.' And again: 'He looked round about Him and said, Who shall do the will of God, these,' saith He, 'are my brethren.' So, then, such as do not the commands of Christ, are not found clothed with his righteousness, are not his disciples ; and that which a man hath not he cannot give to another; and it is clear that no man, nor *Church*, though truly called of God, and as such having the authority of a Church and minister, *can any longer retain that authority* than they retain the power, life and righteousness of Christianity; for the form is entailed to the power and substance, and not the substance to the form. . . . For, seeing nothing makes a man truly a Christian but the life of Christianity, inwardly ruling in his heart, so nothing makes a Church but *the gathering of several Christians* into one body." (*Barclay's Apology*, Prop. X.)

This passage has been constantly appealed to by the advocates of the abolition of Birthright Membership, and by those that have stated that the Membership of the early Society was not a Birthright Membership ; and it has been printed and extensively circulated, and is not even alluded to by J. S. R. We think he ought clearly to show how it can be reconciled with his idea of a " Birthright Membership " in the early Society, and to explain how the Apologist could write such a passage if " from the rise of Friends the children of its members have always been deemed to belong to it."

The whole of Barclay's " Anarchy of the Ranters "[*]

---

[*] A reprint of this work can be procured, price 3d., of W. Irwin, of Manchester. This tract was written at the request of the Morning Meeting, which then consisted of the Founders of the

precludes the possibility of the existence of Birthright
Membership. It is there stated that the Early Friends
were "not so foolish as to concern ourselves with those
who are not of us, far less who stand in opposition to
us, so as to reprove, instruct, or reclaim them as *fellow
members* or brethren."—Page 23.

We would meet the supposed analogy of our membership to that of the Church of England, by the
following quotation from Edward Burrough, stating
the objections of the early Friends to the constitution
of the Church of England.

In a paper which now lies before the writer in
manuscript, Edward Burrough gives "Some few
reasons showing why we deny the Church of England," and are "such as are scornfully called Quakers."
He first states that they consider the Church of England is a "false church," and then gives the reasons
"why she is a false church." The first reason is:
"Because she is not constituted of right members, but
made up of members which *are not born again*, nor
renewed in mind and heart (and of such members
only doth the true Church of Christ consist), but the
Church of England consists of the contrary." He
claims for the Society of Friends, as against the
Church of England, that "this way of religion is
according to the Scriptures, and in the fulfilling of
them (*i.e.* the Scriptures) in doctrine, practice, and
conversation, and the ministry, ordinances, church
government, and discipline," "according to the example of the Apostles."

But the clear and decisive testimony he bears to the
constitution of the early Society of Friends, must
convince the most incredulous that, at that early
period, Birthright Membership was repudiated as a

Early Society, and shows that the Society generally endorsed
the views on Church government there expressed.

mark of a " false church ;" and that young persons, on attaining their majority, were not received as members of the outward Church by right of parentage, as represented by J. S. Rowntree.

E. Burrough continues the reasons why the Society of Friends *is* a true church : " Fifthly. Because we have assurance, through faith, of the love and favour of the Lord God, and have obtained the rest, where comfort and satisfaction is enjoyed and the body of sin put off, and Christ the new man put on ; and our whole church consisteth of such members, and NONE BUT SUCH *are members of our Church,* but who are born again of the seed of God, nor is any in FELLOWSHIP WITH US, but who know something of God in them to guide them."

It will be observed that in this quotation there is no escape. Either Edward Burrough was hypocritically finding fault with the constitution of the membership of the Church of England, and falsely representing that the Society of Friends at that period was constituted on a radically different principle, or our friend, J. S. R., is mistaken in his conclusions.

We venture to consider these two quotations decisive of the question. If they are not, a very heavy charge against the sincerity of the Christian character of our early Friends may be considered to be proved, viz. that what they preached, they did not practise ; and that what they publicly, and in the most solemn manner, attacked as a great evil in the Presbyterian Church and the Church of England, they adopted in their own Society. It will be observed that E. Burrough uses the word " Member," and in "fellowship with us" in a sense which refutes J. S. R.'s theory that in the early Society Attenders were deemed Members, or that Infants were deemed Members.

We will, however, go a little farther, and deal with the reasoning by which points of resemblance are dwelt upon, which have, we venture to think, absolutely nothing to do with the question; and points of difference, which really involve the whole question, are passed lightly over. Our friend says, " From the rise of Friends, the children of its Members have always been deemed to belong to it," therefore, " the statement that Birthright Membership is a modern institution is not sustained." In what sense " *to belong,*" to it ? The whole question of Birthright Membership is a question whether the *government and conduct of a particular Church* should rest, First, with *Christians;* and, Secondly, with persons who *have accepted its rules and methods* of pursuing its great Christian objects. Now the article itself furnishes conclusive evidence that in *this* sense the children of Members were *not* " deemed to belong to it ;" and that a child of a Member, in 1672, had not, on the ground of being a Member's child, the slightest right to participate in its conduct or government ; but that a young man of twenty-one, who was " faithful," " weighty," " seasoned," " substantial," evincing an attachment to the Society, was invited by the Elders, *i.e.* Ministers of the Church, and with the consent of the Monthly Meeting, became entitled to take his seat as a Member.*

J. S. Rowntree has understated the qualifications

---

* As a proof that this was not only the theory but the practice, the reader may refer for a statement of the practice of the Early Society to page 39 of the " Life of Joseph Pike," published by the writer's father John Barclay, who remarks (pages 40 and 41) on this as a decisive proof ; and states that the original membership of the Society was not a Birthright Membership. " So far were our worthy predecessors," " *those who moulded* the Sect of the Quakers " (he is refuting a statement of Beverley's in his " Letters on the State of the Church") from retaining " the worst arrangements of the Church of Rome and the Church of England, or even of the *heathen Brahmins,*" by allowing "the carnal birth of those born merely by

required, because there is in existence a minute of the Yearly Meeting—enacted shortly after 1672, the date of the first Yearly Meeting, although probably in operation long before—clearly showing that originally no persons whatever were to be admitted to a share in the Church power except those who were *thoroughly converted persons, and who, in both their profession and conduct, were Christian men and women.* Now, let us deal with the two parallel columns at page 252, in which, in spite of the admission that there was a line of division, and that certain members had the administrative power in their hands (page 253), he endeavours to show that the position of a young person, the child of a Friend, then, was substantially the same as it is now.

1st. It is assumed, without the slightest attempt at proof,* that the words " profess with," and " belong to," meant identically the same thing on our ancient minute books, &c., and do not mean what the words naturally signify.

2nd. That the marriage with a Friend of a young man twenty-one years of age, at our meeting-houses, in 1672, implied that he was a full member ; when it is well known, that marriages constantly took place at that period, between persons who were Friends and persons who were not strictly Friends, but " professed with " Friends, or objected to marriage by a priest.

7th. Again if such a person died, his burial in a

---

the will of the flesh to enjoy an equal share of all Christian privileges with those who are born of the Spirit." !

The testimony of John Barclay, that this was not "the practice of older and better times," is, the writer submits, entitled to some deference, since, perhaps, no member of the Society of Friends, excepting Sewell, the historian, ever had a more intimate acquaintance with the literature, both printed and manuscript, of the Early Society of Friends.

* See tabular statement at page 252 of J. S. R.'s article in Fourth Month *Quarterly Examiner* of 1872.

Friends' burial-ground proved nothing, because persons, not Friends, were then buried in the said burial-grounds, and that they were used for those who "professed with" as well as those who "belonged to" the Society.

6th. We have before replied to this, which is precisely the point where the whole comparison irretrievably breaks down.

5th. There is no evidence that the Early Friends felt in any way *bound*, in the same manner as we feel bound, by rules and regulations to relieve their own poor ; but if it were otherwise, they extended their relief in special cases by order of the meetings, *even to persons not of the same denomination* as their own.

4th. Here again the proof is wanting that a "paper of denial" was anything more than it purported upon the face of it. A mere attender, if he committed an offence which would bring discredit upon Friends, would be asked to bring in "a paper of condemnation ;" and "a paper of denial" was merely a clearing the Society from any participation in his evil deeds. It is admitted that after the establishment of a distinct Birthright Membership in 1737 the use of these terms ceased, and new terms were substituted : why was this so, if it was coeval with the establishment of the Society ?

3rd. We think it must be admitted on all hands that this is a serious historical error. It is evidently assumed as *conclusive proof* of the fact of Birthright Membership existing in the Society of Friends of 1672, that the Society registered the Births of all their *children*. That is, that after denouncing the baptism of infants, on the ground that they could not be members of a Church,—the same men entered them as Church Members and *little Christians* on the books of the Society ! Let us consider whether we know the reasons for the establishment of the registers of Births, Deaths, and Marriages. Is it not obvious that all persons, whether Friends or not, who objected to have their children baptized by a priest, married by a priest, and buried by a priest, would be cut off, by their non-use of the parish registrars (which were exclusively under the charge of the ecclesiastical authorities) from the proof of their title to property of various kinds, and from all other advantages of such Registers, unless they established registers of their own? It has been assumed that George Fox first conceived this idea; but it is a historical fact that all the Baptist churches, and many of the Independent Societies, who objected equally with Friends to the National Ministry or priesthood, had such registers, prior to the adoption of the plan by G. Fox. Now it must be obvious that if Baptists had their children registered in the register-book of their own Meeting Houses, J. S. R.'s argument would equally prove that the *Baptists had a Birthright Membership* and the children of *their* members were "always deemed to belong to them"—a supposition entirely contrary to the fact; because every Baptist, ancient or modern, has contended for *adult* baptism and Membership, and has objected to the Baptism and reception of children as Members.

And we may further add, as a decisive proof, *that the registration of the infants of Friends had nothing whatever to do with Membership;* and that, at the period of the *first entries,* many Births, Marriages, and Burials, date so far beyond the date of the rise of the Society as to show that the whole registry was not contemplated from the point of view it now appears to present to our friend J. S. R., and that had he examined the original Register Books they would have shown that such a view could not be taken.

It is obvious that, if the earliest Registers of Birth dating from the rise of the Society were intended to be *lists of Members,* they would have contained the date of birth of all adult Members, and this they evidently do not do : and if they were intended to form a list of all the infant Members (if we assume, with J. S. R. for a moment, there was any such intention), the Registers ought to be strictly confined to infants born either *after* the date of the establishment of the Register books, viz. 1668 to 1672, or within the date of the rise of the Society, say from 1652.   We take the List of the Registrar-General, and select a few instances, *e. g.* Ampthill, a Birth register for 1643 ; Langford, 1646 ; Barking, 1632; Cornwall Q. M., 1609 ; East division, 1634 ; Plymouth, 1627 ; Romsey and Southam, 1622 ; Headley and Bramshot, 1638; Colchester, 1613 ; Gainsborough, 1632 ; Kendal, 1617.   There is a Marriage in the Plymouth book for 1646 ; the Monthly Meeting of Aldebury, Beccles, and Heningham register one in 1639 ; Kendal, a Marriage in 1643 ; while at Thirsk a Burial is registered for the year 1610 ! We conclude even J. S. R. would hardly claim the person here registered as a Birthright Member, or as a follower of Fox !   There are large numbers of entries of persons long before the date at which Friends began to acquire Burying Grounds ; and of Births twenty to twenty-five years before the books were established, but not sufficient for us to suppose that on the adhesion of a person to the Society his Birth was registered.

E

CHAPTER IV.

Some remarks on the position of Children in the Christian Church
—The effect of Birthright Membership on the preaching of
the Gospel—A few practical suggestions for the reversion
of the Society to a sound system of Christian Membership—
On the "visible standard of holiness" in the Society of
Friends—Conclusion.

AN instance is given in the paper of the children
of some of the early Friends having kept up the
meetings for worship when all their parents were
in prison. It is truly a touching incident; but it
also is made to serve the necessities of the argument,
and it shows very clearly the way in which two things
essentially distinct are constantly confused in the
Article. "It illustrates," he says, "the power of
those children's faith, and indirectly their relation to
the religious body to which their parents belonged."
The children clearly showed, by their actions,
that they possessed in their hearts the work of faith
with power; they were Members of the Church
Universal, and therefore it is tacitly assumed to be
necessary that they should be *Members* of the early
Society of Friends; and that the noble conduct of
the children was in some way the result of Birthright Membership. The assumption made here, and
elsewhere, is this: that every person who has true
faith shown by works, ought to be, and must be, part
of a visible Church Society; and in order to secure
this end, all the infants born, within certain limits, of
Christian parents, ought to be made to belong to some
outward Church. The Church of Rome, the Church of
England, and the Presbyterian Church thought so, and
endeavoured, unavailingly, to enforce the idea by the
sword. Now is it absolutely necessary to every

Christian that he should join some outward Church ?
" We saw one casting out devils in Thy name," said the
disciples of our Lord, "and we forbad him, because he
followeth not us;" and the reply was, "forbid him not,
for there is no man who can do a miracle in my name
who can lightly speak evil of me;" "He that is not against
us is with us." The early Society of Friends took
the view that a man might belong to the Church Universal, and might even "profess with Friends" without
being a Member of their Society or entrusted with
Church Government. It is this confusion of ideas between the Church Universal, which is *one*, and a Church
or Society in a particular place or places, which leads
our author to the anxiety that children should not be
unchurched. There can be no objection to consider
children, when they have sufficient faith in Christ to
strive to "do the things that He says," as unquestionably belonging to the Church Universal. But what
has this to do with the question of Birthright Membership, even if the text, "all your children are holy,"*
(1 Cor. vii. 14) should be taken to mean all your children are members of the Church Universal and are
regenerate persons ? Our objection to considering them
as members of a particular Church is, that they are not
fit to perform the duties of such a Society. They may
be able to perform certain functions of the Church
Universal, but until they are able to understand their
duties as members of a particular Church, and can
exercise them rightly, the responsibility does not
attach to them. Children are not exhorted in the
New Testament to obey *the officers* of the church, but
to obey their *parents;* while adult Christians are

---

* Upon this text Dean Alford speaks plainly and nobly when he
says, "With regard to the bearing of this verse upon Infant
Baptism, it seems to me to have NONE !" (See Alford's New Test.
in loc.).

exhorted to obey their Church Officers. There is not a *single text* in the New Testament which implies in the remotest degree that infants, or young children, were considered as belonging to the Church, in the sense in which it can be considered as an objective outward society to advance the interests of Christianity.

Children of *Christian* parents are placed by Divine providence in a position in which the responsibility of their religious training rests not upon the Church but exclusively upon the parents. Church officers *cannot* in *any case rightly interfere* between the parents and children. The legitimate deduction from the principles laid down by J. S. R. would be that they can rightly do so. As a deduction from the same principles, in the Church of England the right to catechise the children of a given district was given to the clergy, and had the force of law. All the Church can legitimately do is, we venture to think, this : to enforce on Christian parents their duties, and to offer them, in certain cases, the advantages of Christian Instruction for their children, of a superior kind, to supplement their own. In some cases this may be best done in connection with education, as in our public schools; in other cases it may be done independently.

We see no adequate reason alleged in this article for the alteration of J. S. R.'s views, and we regret that we cannot find a single practical suggestion which seems likely to help the Society of Friends in its difficulties. We believe it is a fact that, as far as the perpetuation of the existence of our Society, the whole apparatus of our Adult Schools and Missions has, to a large extent, merely served to retain our younger Members by causing them to look away from the machinery of our Society, as cumbrous and ill-adapted to the great objects of a Church, and to leave it to go on its way alone and unaided. The maxim, "it will last our time," expresses the strong objection of the human mind to any kind of change, although convinced of its absolute necessity, both on scriptural and rational grounds.

But then what will become of our Missions and Schools? Will they pass over to any other body of Christians, and still under another name retain their force and their usefulness? We think not, and that there are already indications that the gradual closing of our Meeting Houses will be the gradual closing of our Schools and Missions; and that nearly the whole net result to our common Christianity will be the abstraction of so many centres of Christian light and usefulness, and of a large amount of property from the sum total of the means by which a sound and spiritually-minded form of Christianity, uncorrupted by the admixture of the Priestly or Sacramental element, is extended to the general population.

• J. S. Rowntree very rightly remarks that "the working of Meetings for Ministers and Elders" is "worthy of our consideration," and that "few arrangements, civil or religious, in this country, are more elaborate in their machinery," than that which "is required for the appointment of Elders and recording of Ministers;" and he asks "What is the outcome of this elaborate machinery?" The attentive peruser of J. S. Rowntree's Prize Essay, "Quakerism, past and present," will be at no loss, we think, for an answer; and it is, shortly, this: that since the introduction of Birthright Membership and the institution of non-preaching or "Governing" Elders (of which we may remark there exists no mention in the New Testament, and that such officers were also unknown in the early Society of Friends), the Society of Friends as "a Church," (to use the words of its founders) has declined in numbers to an extent which threatens its ultimate extinction both here and in America,* and in a strictly Christian point of view as a Society, has not contributed its quota to the conversion of sinners, and the visible advancement of the Christian religion.

The most serious effect of Birthright Membership is that which it has upon our practical action for the propagation of the Gospel in its simplicity and purity, and on the shepherding of the flock already gathered. There is no visible *flock,* and thus Christian ministers are not acknowledged in their pastoral relation. "Take heed to yourselves and to the *Flock,* over which the Holy Ghost has made you Overseers, to feed the Church of God, which He hath purchased with His own blood." The institution of non-preaching or "Governing" Elders and Overseers,† in the definition which we now make of their duties, was the necessary outcome of Birthright Membership, because it is obvious that after this was instituted there existed no body of persons in our Society who, in the New Testament sense, represented the outward and visible Church, the "Body of Christ," and the "Mind of the Spirit," and therefore in practice it was obviously necessary that there should be a body of persons constituted who should *stand between the mixed Congregation* and the Ministers, and it was so arranged that they did not even *represent* this mixed congregation. Then

---

* It has become practically extinct in Wales, Scotland, and Holland. The correctness of the statements of the writer respecting the rapid decrease of Friends in America, have not hitherto been contested, and have received confirmation from the Clerk of Indiana Yearly Meeting.

† We believe the word "Elder" to have been originally applied exclusively to Ministers. At a Conference lately held at Leeds, certain Early Minutes of Brighouse Monthly Meeting were quoted to show that they were not *always* so. We believe that these Minutes, rightly understood, will be found to refer, not to "Elders," but to "Overseers" or "Deacons," who were not generally Ministers.

duties, which unquestionably belonged to Christian ministers who were chosen by the New Testament Church to fulfil the office of "overseer" or "bishop," were transferred to other persons, who were generally officers for life, and whose duties were loosely defined, and the exercise of them imperfectly controlled, and whose appointment, it might generally be said, had no clear and Scriptural warrant, nor was there evident proof to the Church that "the Holy Ghost *had* made them overseers," and that they themselves felt a distinct call to perform these duties. The oversight of the flock, private religious conversation with them; the encouragement or advice of the younger ministers; the visitation of the sick; the instruction of the children of Members in the truths of the Christian religion where there was the opening for such service; the attempt to form new Meetings where none exist, by the conversion of worldly sinners; the uniting of the younger ministers with themselves in such service; the regular supply of all the congregations of Friends with Ministers, are all matters which fell within the province of such Church Officers, and respecting which they were, we think, *accountable* to the Church. The ancient practice of Ministers giving an account of their proceedings to the Church, on their return from a religious visit with a certificate, is a familiar instance, which proves that Ministers were considered in the early Society of Friends as responsible to the Church. Complaints of the want of a supply of Ministry, from various meetings, may also be mentioned in proof of the existence of this responsibility. Such complaints would now be considered altogether out of place, and evincing a want of dependence upon the great Head of the Church. It is in accordance with natural and spiritual laws that if a trust or office is *confided* to Christian persons who feel *called to undertake it*, that a peculiar and real pleasure will be felt in endeavouring to discharge it, and such persons can then feel that they have a claim on all persons who profess themselves to be Members, for assistance of every kind, spiritual, practical and material,* in their attempt rightly to discharge their duties, and give a good account of their stewardship. Are we, in our anxiety to be free from every vestige of *priestcraft,* and every shred of making, in the words of the Apostle Paul, " godliness a *source of emolument,"* to overthrow the New Testament idea of the Christian Ministry or Eldership, as a *distinct office* of the outward and visible Church ?

Many difficulties which present themselves in view of the abolition of Birthright Membership, would be entirely obviated by the concession of this position to certain Ministers, rightly called and chosen, from time to time, and who would be held responsible to act for each Church in all those things in which *all* Members *cannot rightly act.* We should recollect that although all the Members are necessary, and therefore have a certain equality of rights—yet that Christ, "when He ascended up on high," gave *some* apostles, prophets, evangelists, pastors, and teachers, for the *perfecting of the saints* for the work of the ministry, for the edifying of the body of Christ—and that the Church of Christ acts through and are " fellow-helpers " of such officers. This subject, however, is one on which we do not, at present, intend to enter.†

---

* " And if at any time they be called of God, so as the work of the Lord hinder them from the use of their trades (Ministers) *take what is given them by such to whom they have communicated spirituals."*—Page 294, X. Prop., Barclay's Apology, Baskerville Edition.

† We may, however, remark that there is an universal feeling that our arrangements respecting the Ministry are imperfect and unsatisfactory. Persons whose ministry would never be sanctioned by a majority of the Church continue for years to exercise it to the

It is obvious that J. S. Rowntree's remarks (see page 268, and in note on page 269) tend to the abolition of the New Testament distinction between a person exercising a gift of grace and having to some extent the approval of the Church within the Society, and persons recognised by all as able Ministers, called of God, and therefore invested with the office of "overseer" of "a flock." The distinction is feeble enough already among us from causes which this paper, we trust, clearly points out. If the mere regular attenders of a Christian congregation are to have the rights of professing Members of a Christian Church, the levelling of the distinction between a Church Member and an attender of public worship, will obviously be fatal to a sound Christian Ministry and to the proper carrying out of the responsibilities which attach to the Church Officers, called in the New Testament "Overseers" or "Bishops;" and the Society will know less than ever *where the responsibility lies* for the state of things existing in our Church for the last century and a half, which we believe, in its peculiar character, cannot readily be paralleled in church history, and therefore it will, however earnest or zealous its members may be, be UNABLE to apply a remedy.

It is obviously desirable that Membership in a Christian Church should be on the broadest basis, sanctioned by the largest and most liberal construction of the spirit of the Christian Religion as explained in the

---

injury and discouragement of our congregations, while those whose ministry would be fully approved by a majority of the particular Meeting in which they reside, are for years left in uncertainty whether it is so approved ; and the idea has gained currency that all our members have some inherent right occasionally to preach, under colour of the exercise of "the liberty of prophesying" apart from the sanction of the Church, and also that all preachers of the Gospel ought to *hold office.*

New Testament. Knowing the importance of a proper oversight of the lambs of the flock of Christ—persons in whom consciousness of sin and the need of a Saviour had been awakened by the preaching of the Gospel, John Wesley, with that sound religious experience and accuracy of definition for which he was eminent, laid down a basis for the wider extension of the *privileges* of the Church of Christ and for Christian oversight, by the reception, as members on trial, of all persons who came under the class of those who "felt themselves to be sinners, and were seeking the salvation which is in Christ Jesus," on the sole condition of their regularly attending classes superintended by experienced Christians, for religious instruction and prayer. We ask is this not a basis *broad* enough and *narrow* enough for the extension of Church oversight and privileges apart from the imparting of Church duties and control ?

Let us consider its vast practical utility. Here is a man who has just been turned from his evil ways and is *seeking salvation,* but has not yet found Christ, could not say that he had faith in Christ, or the sense of the presence of the Holy Spirit in his office of the Comforter—needing all the *help* and *guidance* of concerned ministers of the church, but quite *unfit to be received as a Church Member.* The question as to his reception of the principles of the New Testament received by Friends—most important as a basis of agreement for practical and united action—is entirely beside the mark. He may be an attender of our meetings, but it would be absolutely injurious to his religious life to be introduced at this moment into the responsibilities of a Church Member. Among the children of Friends we believe that there are stages of Christian experience in which it may be equally injurious, and that this, in a spiritual point of view, is not compensated by the appointment of young people to trifling and unimportant services.

The great stronghold of Birthright Membership in our Society is—the great desire of decidedly Christian parents to obtain *Christian privileges* for their children ; and the great desire of parents who cannot so be considered that their children should have, without thought or trouble on their part, the advantage of belonging to a Society who, by their judicious care in the extension of a sound moral and religious education by means of public schools and by the exercise of Church discipline, have obtained a high position in public estimation.

If, therefore, we could establish a kind of preliminary or trial membership, on the principle of extending Church privileges to persons "who feel themselves to be sinners and are seeking salvation," *willing of their own accord* to come under religious instruction and oversight, as in the case of the classes in our adult schools, and our Bible-classes, conducted by approved and concerned Ministers or teachers, for the children of our Members, and empower *them* to grant this preliminary Membership, without any formalities, to regular attenders of good character under their instruction and oversight, this would give us an outer circle of persons who, as in the early Society, to some extent "profess with Friends," but who are unprepared to join our Society ; and we should not refuse Christian privileges and instruction to those who, as yet, do not entirely agree with us in opinion. If the Society were further to extend full Membership to all persons who, having been instructed (whether by their parents only, or in our public schools, or in Bible-classes superintended as above described), in the truths of the Christian religion (which would necessarily include all principles whatever which are or ought to be professed by Friends, and which could be found clearly taught in the New Testament), and professing faith, personally or in writing, in the Lord Jesus Christ as *the* Son of

God, and whose daily life and conduct was found to
be in accordance with that profession ;—we think that
the Christian earnestness of many of our younger
Ministers and members would shortly be turned to
good account. Parents would see that *real religious
advantages* would be offered to their children, because
the motives for doing so would be allowed full scope.
Ministers would soon see real and visible fruit of their
labours in the conversion of sinners, and in the blessing
which attends the decided profession of allegiance to
Christ, our dear Lord and Master, by those who are
turned from darkness to light and from the power of
Satan to God. By means of the assistance they would
receive from the younger Ministers, and the labours of
their converts, we cannot doubt but that a long and
useful career would present itself to the Society of
Friends, and it would be made a fit instrument in the
hand of the Great Head of the Church for the purpose
of winning large masses of the skilled mechanics of
this country (who seem to be rapidly falling under the
leadership and instruction of professed infidels), and
also many of the middle-class tradesmen, to a con-
sistent unflinching testimony for Christ and His
Gospel, and that these would soon be seen to form
a very *desirable* addition to our Body. Considering
the extent to which the doctrines and practices of
Roman Catholicism are spreading, and that the
" sacrifice of the mass " to all intents and purposes can
now be offered in the Church of England without legal
restraint, it would appear that a time is approaching
when the simple Christianity of the New Testament
as held by the Society of Friends will obtain—if
the Society desire it—a more favourable hearing, and
that some of the more spiritually-minded members of
the Church of England who, if they join any Society,
now join the Plymouth Brethren, would find scope for
their exertions within our borders.

Something has been said, in one of the public journals devoted to the interests of the Society, about "our title to existence as a Church." We have no title to existence if we cannot show that we are a New Testament Church. But the writer ventures to think that a Society, which alone maintains in this country that all War and all revenge is forbidden under the New Testament dispensation, need not seek far for its " title to existence." Our views respecting the spirituality of the Gospel dispensation, and our rejection of the Priestly element—that the ministry of the Gospel is not the exclusive duty of a clerical or professional class: the propriety of its exercise by women—the advantages of silent as well as vocal prayer and praise—are surely sufficiently important if carried out by men *jealous only for the honour of Christ,* to make good our claim to existence as an independent Christian Church.

When we consider the large number of work-people employed by Members of our Society, we can hardly suppose that we have not a mission to *them*—if to no others—or that the same simple principles of the New Testament may not be equally beneficial to them as to our own children.

A period of Revival has come, and we fear there are already signs of its being on the wane. We have been unable *as a Society* to stretch out our hands and grasp the fruit within our reach. We fear it has not always fallen into good ground and reproduced its kind.

If the obstacles which an erroneous system of Church Membership and Church Officers—at variance with the original intention of the founders of the Society—can be removed, or if the means for working on a Scriptural method of church architecture can be provided—no person acquainted with the means of usefulness at our disposal can doubt that within, comparatively, a few years, our Membership might be doubled, and the glory of God and the salvation of our fellow-men largely promoted; and the great experiment of the practical establishment of churches on the New Testament model which has been called "Quakerism," conducted under the blessing of the Great Head of the Church to a successful conclusion, instead of being *"reproachfully pointed at by those who fear or envy the greatness* of Quakerism!" It is "great" because it is not the religion of the *Priest*; but *if it does not still strive to copy the religion of the New Testament in all its features* it has not only departed from its original object, but we may be sure the axe is laid to its root.

If it be true that "the visible standard of holiness" is higher in the Society of Friends than in other Churches, we think a member of a Church in which membership is dependent upon "personal application" "a profession of faith in Christ," and the visible fruits of such faith, might ask how many persons had, through the agency of our Church, visibly altered their conduct, or evidently embraced Christianity in consequence of their connection with our Society? and whether it was to be expected that a Christian Church which is doing its duty towards the great mass of mankind, and constantly receiving the accession of Members on whom the forces of Christianity have not, by any means, fully exerted their power, should exhibit the same "visible standard of holiness" which prevails in a Society where the advantages of a guarded Christian education are extended to the poorest Members?

We are in danger of forgetting that "He that judgeth us is the *Lord*," and that the rule on which "obvious piety and holiness of life" are to be judged is that "where *much* is given *much will also be required.*"

The writer had once the pleasure of visiting a regularly-constituted Church in London, whose members consisted of costermongers, artificial flower girls, and the lowest class of little shopkeepers, &c. in one of the worst parts of London, most of whom had been changed from a visible form of *un*holiness to some visible measure of holiness. With the help of the person who, by the dedication of his spare time, had, under the guidance of the Holy Spirit, called this Society into being, they are as perfectly able in their measures to administer the affairs of their Church as any of our own Meetings, and have certainly done so as much for the glory of God. But would it not be contrary to every principle of our religion and to right reason to compare their " visible standard of holiness," their " fruit-bearing in matters of obvious piety," with an equal number of the Society of Friends ?

Yet this is really what our friend J. S. R. does (see p. 267) to show that being born into a Society, composed, for the most part, of persons not exposed to a tithe of the temptations which must inevitably fall to the lot of the great mass of the population, produces a higher standard of Christian morality than an opposite system of Membership.

It must be obvious that the very idea that the conditions in life and circumstances of the persons compared must be taken into account, never occurred to our friend; for he states (pp. 267, 268) that in the district where he resides, he has ascertained by the statistics of disownments, that the conduct of persons who have joined the Society by " personal application," or convincement, is *inferior* to that of Birthright Members : forgetting that they have not received the same careful religious teaching, and that their circumstances have generally been in every way less favourable. Not only so, but the Society (accordingt o J. S. R.'s statement, p. 263) does not require any " declaration of faith" in Christ from these persons, but merely that they agree with us in opinion, and are persons of moral conduct; and we can scarcely conceive any condition more favourable than these for the reception of persons who desire to be associated with a Society of high reputation from other than simply Christian motives.

Is not the reputation of the Society of Friends sufficiently accounted for—First, by the influence of their Christian principles; Secondly, by the careful religious training of the children of their members in our public schools; Thirdly, by the fact of an exceedingly small accession to their ranks from the irreligious world, and, prior to the last ten years, from a rigid exercise of the Discipline on our Members, and their removal from many obvious temptations by the public opinion produced by its exercise; and Fourthly, because they are not an aggressive Body? *

"Woe unto you when all men speak well of you," said our Lord to His disciples; and when we are drawing comparisons between our own "holiness of life" and that of our fellow-Christians, we cannot be too diffident of the extent of our knowledge, or the accuracy of our judgment. It might be asked, for instance, whether the pecuniary self-denial and privation of the Society, in proportion to its means, for the maintenance and propagation of the Christian religion, are not incomparably smaller than those voluntarily and cheerfully borne by the Free Churches of this country? and whether a man's spirituality of mind, and the fervour of his attachment to Christ, are or are not in any way to be measured by the sacrifices he makes for the promotion of His cause? We have amongst us particular instances of noble Christian

---

* To this may be added the influence of race, and a long line of ancestors untainted by vice.

self-devotion, but let us admit that so have other churches.

" Ye are the *light of the world,*" said our blessed Lord to His disciples; and truly the Christian, whether in a palace or a prison, whether alone or in the world, is *a* light reflecting the beams of his Light and Sun. Are we, therefore, to stand *alone* " as lights in the world ?" Such a system may be "eminently successful in stamping the sense of personal (or rather *individual*) responsibility " upon a few persons of pre-eminent intellectual and moral qualifications ; but it is not the Divine system, nor that revealed by the conduct of our Lord and His apostles. He *chose twelve.* He was himself with them, as " one who serveth," but yet as their outward Overseer or Shepherd. The Apostles acted on the same principle ; and overseers or bishops, with various "gifts of grace," are described as acting as under-shepherds of the flock, of which Christ is the " Chief Shepherd."

We have done ; but we would ask our readers to consider the last portion of the text, " Ye are the light of the world, a *city* set on a hill *cannot be hid,*" and we would ask where would be this " light" of the world, and this " city," if there was no outward and visible distinction between the professed disciples of Christ and the world ? Is it not their *visible union* which makes them " *the* light of the world," and " a city." If the mere attendance at a place of worship, and moral conduct, makes a man a member of the outward and visible Church, it is obviously an invisible " city," and there is no outward mark to distinguish its citizens from those who are not " the light of the world." The struggle between the Martyrs of the Christian Church and the powers of the world, was visibly and outwardly between their previous profession of faith in Christ and their promise " to live and fight as a soldier of Christ and of God," and the renouncement of that profession and that promise. Was this not intended by our Lord, who " knew what was in man," to be an additional strength in the fearful moment of their trial ? An outward and visible point was given by it to the struggle between Christ's Religion and the World, and one capable of being apprehended by the coarsest and vilest of men. There is now, in a different form, an equally violent spiritual struggle, and human nature and the Religion of Christ requires that it shall have an outward and visible form. It is against this *visible form of* PROFESSED ALLEGIANCE *to Him* in which Christ has moulded His Church that this struggle is raging in the world, and in the bosom of Societies which profess themselves to be Churches. It is desired to reduce Christianity to the level of a *mere School of Opinion,* and to remove from it the element of outwardly professed loyalty to Him as shown by vigorous and united action in outward Societies. This is as far removed from Sectarianism as light is from darkness.

The motto of the great Enemy of Christ and His Gospel is, " Divide and conquer." The maxim of all the Apostles and leaders of His Church has been to unite the scattered sheep, who are but too prone to wander alone instead of seeking the Good Shepherd's care in a closer Christian communion. " That which we have seen and heard declare we unto you, that ye also may have fellowship with us, and truly our fellowship is with the Father and with his Son Jesus Christ." The whole world is invited to partake of this Christian Communion," which is the possession of " the Church of God which He hath purchased with his own blood."

This " Church " was not an abstract or " ideal " conception, but was a particular Society in a given place, with definite officers, and with " a restricted Membership." It was not, we conceive, a Christian

Communion,* like earthly friendship, " so delicate and subtle in its manifestations," that it is only occasionally experienced in " the most select companies of saintly persons," which so many of our most valued Members are seeking, but something far more practical and attainable. It is merely this, that our terms of Christian Communion shall be made neither broader nor narrower than that of the Church of the Apostles.

They believe that the decline of our Society in numbers has been mainly due to the introduction of an Hereditary Membership, and to the measures which necessarily followed this insidious and fatal error.

They do not find that these changes in the original constitution of our Society were dictated by the same high-minded and uncompromising adherence to the noble and practical ideal of the revival of " primitive and Scriptural Christianity," possessed by its Founders, but think they see in them traces of human policy and worldly expediency.

They believe that what is truly right must be for a Christian Church truly expedient, and that, therefore, all those who influence the conduct of our affairs should consider in what way this change can be wisely and judiciously made.

NOTE.—Two of our Mission efforts have adopted a Membership founded on a credible profession of faith

---

* The writer may perhaps refer to a paper he read at a Meeting held at Devonshire House, for the discussion of the subject of providing a Membership for our Mission Meetings, on 13th of Twelfth Month, 1869, endeavouring to correct the idea that Christian Communion involved a kind of choice, intellectual and social intercourse. It was printed in the *Monthly Record* of First Month 15th, 1870.

in Christ as the Son of God. In both of these cases it has been established for several years. They are increasing rapidly in numbers, and those who conduct them express their unqualified satisfaction with the growth in grace of these members. In both instances the members exercise a Church discipline in a satisfactory manner.

R. BARRETT & SONS, Printers, 13, Mark Lane, London.